Grar
Rain Song

by Dawn McMillan
illustrated by Richard Hoit

Harcourt
SCHOOL PUBLISHERS

Printed in Mexico

ISBN 10: 0-15-350405-6
ISBN 13: 978-0-15-350405-1

Ordering Options
ISBN 10: 0-15-350332-7 (Grade 2 Below-Level Collection)
ISBN 13: 978-0-15-350332-0 (Grade 2 Below-Level Collection)
ISBN 10: 0-15-357432-1 (package of 5)
ISBN 13: 978-0-15-357432-0 (package of 5)

2 3 4 5 6 7 8 9 10   050   15 14 13 12 11 10 09 08 07

Fay came home from school.
"Katie is singing at the school
show," she said.

"Why don't you sing, too?"
asked Mom.
"I don't like singing," Fay
replied. "I don't know *what* I
can do."

"I have an idea," said Grandma.
"You could play the piano. I'll
teach you a song about the rain."

After dinner, Fay and Mom listened to Grandma play the piano. Fay tapped her knee to the song.

"I played this song at *my* school show," smiled Grandma.

Every night Fay practiced
Grandma's song.

"Good!" said Grandma. "You are doing well."

SCHOOL SHOW

At last, it was time for the show.
Fay whispered, "Grandma, I'm
afraid I'll forget the song."

"Imagine a million drops of rain coming down," said Grandma. "Then you will remember how to play."

Fay felt the curve of the piano
lid. She lifted it and began to
play. Grandma's song danced
from the piano, just like drops
of rain.

After the show, Mom and
Grandma said, "We're proud
of you, Fay!"

Fay laughed. "Grandma's song is the best song in the world!" she said.

Think Critically

1. What was Fay's problem? How did Grandma help Fay?

2. What did Grandma tell Fay when Fay was afraid before the show?

3. How do you think Fay felt after the show?

4. How did you think Fay would do in the show? Why?

5. Would you like to be in a show? Why or why not?

 **Social Studies**

Write a Letter Write a letter from Fay to Grandma thanking her for her help.

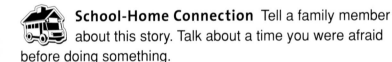 **School-Home Connection** Tell a family member about this story. Talk about a time you were afraid before doing something.